Robin Hood

EVE NICOL

Nicol McNichol
GLASGOW

For my cousins.

*With acknowledgement to
Paul Brotherston, Howard Pyle,
John Hughes, Chris Columbus,
Stephen Spielberg and Stephen King.*

A note on the text

In the original production, the role of LJ was
performed in British Sign Language, translated from
the text here by Amy Helena and Jamie Rae. The
production also featured new songs by Lauren
Gilmour and Audrey Tait for Novasound.

Future productions are encouraged to adapt the text to
their own casts and audiences.

Pack the show full of your favourite 80s pop songs,
write new tunes, or contact Novasound to licence their
synth-sational compositions via www.novasound.net

Robin Hood was commissioned by Cumbernauld Theatre Company and premiered at Lanternhouse, Cumbernauld on 3 December 2021.

LJ   Amy Helena
ROBIN   Julia Murray
SCARLETT   Chiara Sparkes
TUCK   Rosalind McAndrew
SARGE   Lauren Ellis-Stelle

Director   Fiona Mackinnon
Composer   Novasound
Set & Costume   Alisa Kalyanova
Lighting Design   Benny Goodman
BSL Consultant   Jamie Rae
Assistant Director   Amy McCombes
Stage Manager   Rachel Pryde
Deputy Stage Manager   Nina Madriz

Robin Hood

ACT 1

A RADIO BROADCAST

As the audience enter the theatre, a radio broadcasts a cheesy local radio station. Between the adverts for local services and pop classics, the host takes calls from the residents of Greenwood; bunions, sightings of a large beast in the woods and the power outages that have been blighting the town. Just as the calls start to get interesting, there is a huge spark as the radio short circuits out with a spark. In the flash, the shadow of a colossal shaggy beast is seen and a low growl like thunder rumbles through the space.

And is gone.

MEET THE GANG

Wow, look at this. At the outskirts of Greenwood, a green belt New Town, is Robin's gang hut. This is everything you ever wanted. Sitting proudly in the centre of the woods like the playset of your dreams. Part Ewok village, part building site, this is the gang hut. It's been built and updated in wood pallets, scaffolding and old shopping trolleys over time. It's held together with spit and the indestructible spirit of childhood. It's multi-layered with different sections for dancing, band practice, feasts or just chilling out. The personalities of the gang shine through in bits of decoration here and there. It's a monument to their friendship and fun.

LJ looks at it fondly. She's dressed in hand-me downs, not sure of her own style. The eternal good kid. Someone your mum would be happy for you to play with.

LJ. *(to the audience)* Everyone has their own version of what happened that Christmas. I've heard just about every explanation. It was climate change, mass delusion, something in the water, 5G signals. Once, I told my mum what happened. And she laughed. I laughed, of course I was joking. Wasn't I? There are only five of us who know what really happened. This is what good kids do, right? "Always tell the truth". You might think it's just one more story amongst all the other stories, but it will at least it'll be out there. The truth is out there.

> *The gang hut starts to come to life as we see the SCARLETT and TUCK tuning their instruments. ROBIN strides up to the front of the band.*

LJ. Our fort was a place where we could make our own rules. Our own little world. And at the centre of our universe -

ROBIN. I am Robin Hood and we are Robin Hood and The Mystery Machine!

SCARLETT. One two three four!

> *The gang play a badass tune. They're really getting into it.*

> *Until the power sparks and blows.*

POWER OUTS

TUCK. Great Scott!

LJ. What was that?

ROBIN. Guess we're just too much to handle.

LJ. It's getting dark.

ROBIN. We don't need power to jam, right guys?

LJ. Give it up, Rob. It'll be getting dark soon. Ouch.

> *LJ's tripped up on something.*

ROBIN. You alright?

LJ. Man. Mum won't be pleased.

ROBIN. Show me.

LJ rolls up her jeans.

ROBIN. Oh yeah. That'll bruise nicely.

LJ shrugs it off.

TUCK. What we gonna do about the kit?

SCARLETT. Do you reckon it's The Beast of Greenwood?

TUCK. Aw quit it.

ROBIN. Beast of Greenwood?

SCARLETT. You'll have missed all this when you were in the city.

ROBIN. What is it?

SCARLETT. It's brilliant.

TUCK. It's a story to scare babies.

SCARLETT. Been all over the local news. Power outs across Greenwood and every time there's been a sighting of THE BEAST!

ROBIN. No way!

SCARLETT. Way. Telling ya. Mercury in retrograde.

TUCK. It's always Mercury with you.

SCARLETT. How would you explain the strange appearance of an unnatural, all powerful, child hungry beast amongst us then?

TUCK. There ain't no beast.

LJ. I saw it down by the train tracks.

SCARLETT. The train tracks?

TUCK. No you never.

LJ. Did so.

ROBIN. What was it like.

LJ. Um... big... no ... huge. Fur all over. Like a feral cat.

ROBIN. Go on.

TUCK. You don't believe this.

SCARLETT. Shh.

LJ. It was a shadow at first. Long and dark. Sparks flew from its eyes. As it flew towards me, I could feel this deep rumble in my belly and the ground start to shake.

SCARLETT. Oooh!

TUCK. If you're just going to tell bootleg Goosebumps I'm going home. *(to Robin)* Dad's making spaghetti and meatballs.

ROBIN. Can I come?

TUCK. Dad said to say "there's always a place at our table for you".

ROBIN. Sweet. See you guys back out here tomorrow?

SCARLETT. What about the batteries bugging out?

ROBIN. Me and Tuck can lift a couple from the shop on our way to the spagfest.

LJ. You're gonna get caught.

ROBIN. No one can lay a hand on Robin Hood. We gotta be ready for the Greenwood Gala!

LJ. You're here for that?

ROBIN. Wouldn't miss it for the world.

SCARLETT. Yeeees!

ROBIN. Top ticket prize on the line.

TUCK. What're we gonna do with it?

SCARLETT. Crystals!

TUCK. Pick and mix!

LJ. Maybe Robin would want to save it.

ROBIN. Pfft. Where's the fun in saving when you can go on a spending spree up the shopping center. Hey, you guys seen that woman getting into everybody's business round The Center?

TUCK. Sticks out like a sore bum.

SCARLETT. Stuck her foot out in front of my solar powered roller skates.

LJ. She burst my bubble gum!

TUCK. Bought the last Krispy Kreme and ate it right in front of me. Everyone in Greenwood knows that I clear out the Krispy Kremes. That's my thing.

ROBIN. Who does she think she is?

TUCK. My dad says she's working for the Corporation. Everyone makes throwing up noises at the mention of 'The Corporation'.

LJ. Yuck.

ROBIN. That'd explain a lot.

TUCK. My dad says they're all a bunch of lizards.

SCARLETT. She's not from around here anyway. No one in Greenwood could afford a digital watch like that.

ROBIN. Oh, you mean this watch?

> *ROBIN gleefully dangles a very spangly wristwatch in front of them.*

TUCK. By the power of Greyskull!

SCARLETT. Robin!

LJ. Did you steal that?

ROBIN. She's not going to miss it. She can buy a new one. Rob from the rich and give to the poor eh?

> *ROBIN slips on the watch.*

SCARLETT. Jinkies!

ROBIN. What's up?

SCARLETT. My Scarlett-senses are tingling. It's that Corporation woman. Coming this way!

ROBIN. Ho ho ho!

> *The gang get out skipping ropes, hand clapping games, comics. Acting all innocent and sweet. ROBIN's head deep in the dressing up box.*

LJ. Rob - Rob - what're you doing?

ROBIN. I'm gonna talk to her. It'll be brilliant.

TUCK. Oh my god. You are crazy, man!

LJ. Is that a good idea?

ROBIN. Let's find out.

HELLO SARGE

Not a hair out of place, officious and polished down to the last inch, is SARGE. Looking distinctly out of place, she trundles a natty looking trolley behind her loaded with gadgets. The Ghostbusters meet the Avon lady. She peers over her fancy aviator shades at the gang with a curl of distaste.

The gang line up like a spot inspection to receive her.

SARGE. Hello, younglings.

ALL. Good afternoon, ma'am.

SARGE. On behalf of The Corporation, I have questions which you are obliged to answer.

ALL. Yes, ma'am.

SARGE. I have centred my rounds round The Centre and the roundabouts roundabout central round here.

SCARLETT. Making me dizzy.

SARGE. I've spoken to your parents.

LJ. Aw shit.

SARGE. But my readings suggest the answers lie with Greenwood's criminal wannabes. Anything strange in your neighbourhood.

SCARLETT. Other than Tuck?

TUCK. Go play in traffic.

SARGE. Focus, kids.

TUCK. Ignore my associate, ma'am. It's a full moon tonight.

SCARLETT howls and scratches behind her ear.

TUCK. No, ma'am there has been nary a whiff of unusalment in Greenwood until those darn power cuts wiped out all our fun. I'd gotten one thousand on Space Invaders when -

LJ. You never got a thousand.

TUCK. Did too.

SARGE. Space Invaders you say?

LJ. It's a game.

SCARLETT. It's trash.

TUCK. My dad says its a classic.

SCARLETT. A classic waste of time.

SARGE. Any other uncommon occurrences?

TUCK. LJ saw something by the train tracks.

SARGE is interested. She takes out a notepad. SCARLETT digs her elbow into TUCK's ribs.

SARGE. Go on.

LJ. Um... well...

SCARLETT now elbows LJ.

SCARLETT. What you doing?

LJ. But...

SCARLETT. You don't need to say anything LJ.

LJ. But she's an adult.

> *SARGE. bears down on LJ.*

SARGE. As a representative of The Corporation you are obliged to give information to me when requested.

LJ. Ehh...

TUCK. Wait until you hear, ma'am. I pee-ed my pants just hearing about it.

LJ. There was... um... a... by the... ehh..

> *SARGE flips the notebook shut sensing a dead end.*

SARGE. Useless. *(to Tuck)* You there. You have a spark of smart about you.

TUCK. Well, observed, ma'am.

SARGE. A healthy appetite for authority?

TUCK. Starving, ma'am.

SARGE. You wouldn't be also be chummy with a human child about your size... rodent faced... dirty fingers ...

> *ROBIN saunters in dressed in a trench coat, trilby and dark Ray-bans.*

ROBIN UNDERCOVER / PICKPOCKETING

ROBIN. *(putting on a deep voice)* What's going on?

SARGE. Sir.

ROBIN. Are you harassing these upstanding young citizens?

SARGE. I'm here on official Corporation business. And you are...

ROBIN. I'm this cherub's dad.

TUCK. Hey!

ROBIN. Shut your cake hole, my darling angel.

> *SCARLETT puts her hand over TUCK's mouth and drags her away from SARGE. The gang use the distraction of the disguise as an opportunity get to work. Whilst ROBIN has SARGE.'s attention, a small conveyor belt of daylight robbery goes on.*
>
> *Treats, snacks and gadgets are being lifted off of SARGE.'s trolly and person.*

SARGE. I'm responsible for locating the source of the of the funny going-ons going on.

ROBIN. Go on...

SARGE. Strange business with the power. Cuts, surges. There's been gossip around town about "a beast". Ha ha ha ha ridiculous. Nothing more than vandalism I say.

ROBIN. Who on earth would besmirch our pleasant town?

SARGE. There are some real prize assholes in Greenwood. One of them made off with my timepiece.

ROBIN. That'll be that Robin Hood.

SARGE. *(making a note in her book)* Robin. Hood?

ROBIN. She runs this town. Daring. Fast. Ravishing eyes. You got a problem, you track her down. Leave these seraphim be.

SARGE. This Hood sounds like they will be trouble.

ROBIN. The best kind.

SARGE sniffs the air.

SARGE. Is that bubble gum I can smell?

ROBIN. Anything else I can do for you, "ma'am"?

SARGE makes to check her watch, momentarily forgetting it's missing. Sighs.

SARGE. You wouldn't happen to have the time, sir?

ROBIN ostentatiously flourishes her wrist.

ROBIN. I'd say it's coming up for high noon.

SARGE. Thank you. Have a good day, sir. *(Under her breath)* What a wack job.

Robbery complete, ROBIN tips her hat to SARGE and makes to saunter off.

SARGE looks about her but realises she's lost her clipboard, pen, hat, sunglasses. That watch looked awfully familiar...

SARGE. Somebody stop that wack job!

SARGE gives chase to ROBIN who bombs it off stage, throwing her disguise off behind her.

TUCK. Bye, daddy!

SWEARING AN OATH

LJ. *(to the audience)* We made the rules in Greenwood! Or, Robin did. With our input. But they were good rules. Fair.

> *TUCK is making to pocket some of the stash. SCARLETT stays her hand.*

SCARLETT. Oi. Don't forget the pact.

TUCK. *(acquiescing)* Everyone gets an equal share.

SCARLETT. Everyone has a good time, all the time.

TUCK. No one gets left behind.

SCARLETT. Friends until the end of the universe.

TUCK. Swear on your sister's life?

SCARLETT. No problem there, I still haven't forgiven her for my using my dream catcher as a pasta strainer.

ROBIN. Gave that phoney loser the slip around the indoor boules. Didn't I say it'd be brilliant?

SCARLETT. Great job, Rob!

TUCK. Can we dig in now?

ROBIN. Not until we've recited the pact.

ALL. I pledge allegiance to the flag. To always help others and do my best. To boldly go where no one has gone before. By the power of Greyskull. Thunder, thunder, thunder, Thundercats ho. Forever and ever, amen.

EXAMINING THE LOOT

ROBIN. What we looking at here?

SCARLETT has a walkie talkie pinched from SARGE. and tips out the batteries.

SCARLETT. Double As. Two of them.

LJ pulls out a torch.

ROBIN. Oh yeah! Now we're talking.

LJ has unscrewed the torch and slipped out the batteries.

TUCK. Woah! What a haul!

ROBIN. Brand name! We can have a proper jam session with these in the gear.

SCARLETT. Anyone hungry?

SCARLETT empties out a waterfall of goodies from her pockets.

TUCK. Wow!

LJ. Score!

ROBIN. Okay. Huddle up and we'll divide the spoils.

TUCK. M&Ms! Dibs on the blue ones.

SCARLETT. They're exactly the same, weirdo.

TUCK. The blue ones taste bluier.

SCARLETT slides her blue ones over to TUCK.

PLACING A BET

TUCK. Hey, Scarlett. I bet you a mini Mars bar you can't beat Robin to the hill and back.

SCARLETT. Only a dope would take that bet. Robin always wins.

ROBIN. I'd get to the hill and back faster than Tuck could say "amen" over a roast turkey on Christmas.

TUCK. *(hurt)* Hey.

ROBIN. LJ, you gonna race?

LJ. *(to Robin)* Can I have a word, bud?

TUCK. We gotta bet on something or else or its no fun.

SCARLETT. Fine. How many mini Mars bars for second place?

TUCK. Two mini Mars Bars.

ROBIN. *(to LJ)* Later, bud.

SCARLETT. Two mini Mars Bars and a Pepsi and I'm in.

TUCK. Done.

ROBIN. Great. Ready. One

SCARLETT. Diana, goddess of the hunt, be with me...

ROBIN. ... two

TUCK. You're gonna eat my behind, Scarlett.

ROBIN. ... THREE!

> *They race off, but LJ holds ROBIN back.*

ROBIN. Woah! Are you trying to take my head off?

LJ. How are you?

ROBIN. Fine.

LJ. Really?

ROBIN. Fine. Really! It was a real snoozefest in the city. Much rather be here with you dorks.

LJ. Ok.

ROBIN. That it?

LJ. I'm worried abut you. You've been getting into more trouble lately –

ROBIN. Quit dusting my buns, LJ.

SCARLETT bursts back in.

SCARLETT. Winner! Thank you Diana! Wait – were you two even racing?

ROBIN. Nah.

SCARLETT. What're you talking about?

ROBIN. Nothing.

TUCK comes in panting.

TUCK. Second! I got second! Two mini Mars bars and a Pepsi please, Scarlett.

SCARLETT. Whatever, goober.

TUCK. Ha! Where's your Princess Di now?

ROBIN. Hold up. The prize was for second place. You came last Tuck.

TUCK. What!

SCARLETT. Robin and LJ weren't racing.

TUCK. Oh brother. How is that even fair?

> *TUCK passes the goodies back to SCARLETT. SCARLETT gratefully chucks ROBIN one of the Mars Bars. SCARLETT takes a bite out of her bar and casually gives the rest to TUCK and passes the Pepsi to LJ.*

DISCOVERING PIPSQUEAK

> *ROBIN counts out the rest of the stash. One for you, one for you, one for you. Every so often, a small pink paw comes up from behind a box and sneaks away a treat from the piles of treats. None of the gang notice it but they do see something's amiss with the size of their stash piles.*

SCARLETT. Wait. Hold it. Count again. That's not right.

ROBIN. We had more than this. Everyone hand your share back in.

TUCK. No way. These are mine!

SCARLETT. Someone's sneaking extra.

TUCK. Don't look at me.

ROBIN. Come on, we'll count again.

> *The same as before, the piles get smaller and smaller. LJ notices a small furry something out of the corner of her eye and jumps up.*

LJ. Eeek!

TUCK. Popped your puss on a nettle?

LJ. No. Guys. There's something over there.

ROBIN. What's up, LJ?

LJ. A thing. I saw a thing.

ROBIN. What?

LJ. Something hairy.

ROBIN. That Sarge back again?

TUCK. Maybe there's been another escape from the wildlife park?

LJ. No. No. This doesn't look like anything on earth.

SCARLETT. You're freaking me out, LJ.

ROBIN. Are you playing, LJ?

TUCK. She's trying to distract us to get more than her share.

LJ. Look!

> *They all turn round and manage to catch the fuzzy, furry edge of something.*

ALL. Ahhhhhhhh! It's The Beast!

LJ. Guys, shush! You'll scare it.

ROBIN. Did we all see the same thing?

ALL. Uh huh. Yeah.

ROBIN. Okay. Tuck?

TUCK. Yeah boss?

ROBIN. Gimme your M&Ms.

TUCK. LJ, give Robin your M&Ms.

ROBIN. It's only taking the blue ones.

TUCK. But I like the blue ones. Hey!

> *SCARLETT takes the sweets from TUCK and hands them to ROBIN. ROBIN arranges them in a neat pile in plain sight. She stands back and loudly says -*

ROBIN. Oh guys. Was that The Beast over here? Come on. Let us all go all the way over there and see what we can find.

TUCK. What you on about, Robin? The Beast's over there.

> *LJ and SCARLETT put their hands over TUCK's mouth and huckle her off. The gang hide behind a crate. Everything is quiet.*

SCARLETT. Maybe we imagined it. Ate some funny berries?

LJ. Look!

> *A small fuzzy creature is merrily munching away at the pile of M&Ms.*

TUCK. Oh my god oh my god oh my god.

SCARLETT. Is that...

LJ. The Beast!

ROBIN. On three we instigate Action Plan Bundle. OK?

LJ. Okay, alright.

SCARLETT. Got it.

TUCK. Oh my god.

ROBIN. One ... two ...

TUCK. Bundle!

TUCK has gone early and has pounced on the creature.

ROBIN. Oh brother. Tuck!

An almighty battle is taking place between girl and fluff-ball. But TUCK is loosing the battle.

SCARLETT. It's killing Tuck!

LJ. What do we do?

TUCK is screaming bloodcurdling screams.

ROBIN. THREE!

ALL. Bundle!

They storm on top of TUCK and the creature and manage to wrestle it. One by one they peel back. Until just TUCK is rolling on the floor laughing.

SCARLETT. It's not fighting back.

ROBIN. What's it's deal?

LJ. It's tickling!

TUCK. Oh hahaha haha! Stop! Please! Ahaha!

LJ. Geez, I couldn't handle that.

ROBIN swoops up some M&Ms and dangles it in front of the creature. It's distracted and jumps up for it.

ROBIN. Here boy, come on.

We get a good look at the creature. Small, round, big eyes and ears. Undeniably adorable and not a threat at all. It wibbles and blinks.

TUCK. Aww. I was enjoying that. Felt all tingly.

LJ. Tingly?

TUCK. Like licking a battery.

ROBIN. It's cool, gang. This Pipsqueak only wants his share of the spoils.

SCARLETT. Is this... thing... really what the Sarge is looking for?

TUCK. It's not getting any of my sweets. My dad says you shouldn't feed wild animals.

ROBIN. Could this little guy really be messing with the power?

LJ. It's so small.

SCARLETT. Must be.

LJ. And cute!

TUCK. How're we gonna get it to the Sarge?

SCARLETT. What you jabbering about?

TUCK. There's a reward. My dad said The Corporation's getting desperate.

ROBIN. I dunno.

TUCK. Could get us some better gear. Wouldn't have to keep risking our necks to nabs some double As

SCARLETT. Maybe...

LJ. Wait, look.

PIPSQUEAK has started to glow and pulse. Some of the lights in the camp start to power up and the boom box cracks on.

SCARLETT runs over to the keyboards.

SCARLETT. Outrageous! The batteries aren't even in.

LJ. Did it do that?

ROBIN. That's amazing!

TUCK. That's freaky, man.

SCARLETT. We've got power!

ROBIN. Hey, Pipsqueak. Did you do this?

PIPSQUEAK looks quizzically up at ROBIN. Cowering slightly.

ROBIN. LJ. You try. Ask it if it did this.

LJ. Hey little fella.

PIPSQUEAK perks up. Stares at LJ.

ROBIN. Guys, look. LJ's talking to it!

LJ. Did you turn our power on?

PIPSQUEAK stares.

LJ. Maybe. One flash for no. Two flashes for yes?

PIPSQUEAK stares.

TUCK. Oh no. It's thick.

SCARLETT. Shh.

LJ. Do you understand?

TUCK. I told you...

PIPSQUEAK flashes twice.

ALL. Woah!!!

SCARLETT. Now that's wizard.

LJ. Can you power our stuff?

PIPSQUEAK flashes twice.

LJ. It said yes!

TUCK. Coincidence! It doesn't understand. Look. Let me try. Hey Pipsqueak. Can I have your M&Ms.

One flash.

SCARLETT. Oooooh! Burn!

TUCK. Whatever.

ROBIN. You're alright, pipsqueak.

TUCK. It's rabid. Hand it over to the Sarge.

LJ. No way!

ROBIN. Are you kidding? Imagine what we can achieve with Pipsqueak in our gang! No more having to shoplift for our suppers, plugging 50ps into the meter, getting blasted for running up lecky bills. We've got our very our pocket sized dynamo right here.

LJ. And he's smells of bubblegum!

ROBIN. He's bubblegum scented!

PIPSQUEAK purrs at TUCK.

TUCK. Fine.

ROBIN. Guys! Do you know what this means? Robin Hood and The Mystery Machine are back in business!

ROBIN'S HOME IS LOST

SARGE enters with a massive roll of caution tape and begins aggressively masking off areas of the gang hut. The gang hurriedly hide PIPSQUEAK in a backpack and keep him hidden from SARGE.

SCARLETT. Quick! Hide the goods!

LJ. And Pipsqueak.

ROBIN. Sarge can't know we've got him. She'd skin him!

TUCK. Hello again, ma'am.

SARGE. I'm afraid this place is out of bounds to you lot.

ALL. What!

SARGE. It's a hazard.

SARGE. tinkles on a keyboard. Suspicious.

SARGE. Nice keys. How'd you get power out here?

TUCK. Batteries.

SARGE. Batteries, huh.

ROBIN. What do you care?

SARGE. Let me tell you something, punk. I'm no stranger to the harmonic sequence of tones. I could play a tune that would make meteors weep it was so beautiful. But I got myself a real job. Making stones cry is nothing compared to having a job title. And with it, I actually have some influence over the world.

ROBIN. When I grow up, I will never be as bitter as you.

SARGE. You wait.

> *PIPSQUEAK rattles in the bag. TUCK struggles to hold it together.*

TUCK. Woah!

SARGE. What've you got there?

SCARLETT. Nothing, ma'am.

SARGE. Doesn't sound like nothing.

TUCK. We're going to play a set at the gala, ma'am. I'm practicing my solo. Woah!

SCARLETT. Stop. Singing.

SARGE. You're the one they call Tuck.

TUCK. Yeah, ma'am. I'm kinda famous round here.

SARGE. Strange name for a child.

TUCK. It's a cool bad ass nickname.

SARGE. Nick? Name?

SCARLETT. At the end of year disco, she boogied out the loos with her skirt tucked into her tights.

TUCK. Shut up!

ROBIN. Played a whole gig with a breeze round her bum.

LJ. Everyone saw her pants.

TUCK. Still managed to slay the set, didn't I?

ROBIN. She punches us whenever we call her Skid. We settled on Tuck instead.

SARGE finishes putting tape up around the gang hut.

SARGE. Disgusting creatures.

TUCK. Don't worry though ma'am. I'll have my knickers strapped on tight for our performance at the Greenwood gala.

SARGE. Oh no. You delinquents have had the run of things for too long. Until I nix the power problem, The Corporation will provide the gala entertainment

TUCK. What?

SCARLETT. Gross.

LJ. No!

ROBIN. That's our patch!

SARGE. It's right I integrate with the locals. Get some boots on the ground.

ROBIN. Only boots on this ground are mine! Who put you in charge?

SARGE. I come from a higher authority. Oh, and girls. Don't forget to get your mummy and daddy's permission to attend the gala. The Corporation will be enforcing a strict policy on adult supervision. We need to keep your delicate little bones safe until we've tracked down the beastly culprit and restored power. Good bye, whelps.

ALL. *(expect Robin)* Good bye, ma'am.

SARGE. Batteries... interesting...

SARGE stalks off.

PRACTISE IS CANCELLED

They pull PIPSQUEAK out of the bag, he looks a little ruffled.

TUCK. She knew we were hiding something.

ROBIN. She wouldn't know poop if a dog squatted in front of her.

SCARLETT. My horoscope said today was going to be a stinker. I guess practise is cancelled.

ROBIN. You're gonna let that moron win?

TUCK. She has tape, Robin. Tape!

ROBIN. And? When has that stopped us?

SCARLETT. She's something else, Robin. She gives me real bad vibes.

TUCK. Oh go suck a crystal.

SCARLETT. I usually pick up people's karma. With her - zilch.

LJ. Let's just go home.

ROBIN. No one's going home. Robin and The Mystery Machine are going to the gala.

LJ. She'll gut us if she sees you.

ROBIN. I'm not going to let some jerk with a clipboard tell me what to do.

LJ. She's an adult.

ROBIN. And?

LJ. Adults only ever do what they think is best.

ROBIN. Come off it, LJ. When has a loser in a lanyard ever looked out for the little guy. Only way bullies like that learn is to stand up to them.

LJ. But how can we all get in without Sarge spotting Robin?

SCARLETT. Our new buddy could be some help. He's got good juju.

   PIPSQUEAK rocks happily.

TUCK. I can't be bothered.

SCARLETT. Leave the scaredy cats behind then, come on Rob.

LJ. Wait for me.

SCARLETT. Nice one, LJ. Let's get concocting.

ROBIN. No. It's all of us or none of us.

TUCK. You always get us in trouble, Robin.

SCARLETT. That's the whole point.

ROBIN. What's the matter, Tuck? You chicken?

TUCK. Nobody calls me chicken.

SCARLETT. My horoscope told me today was gonna be a good day!

ROBIN. Alright guys. Paws in.

ALL. Friends til the end of the universe.

ROBIN. Let's hit it!

THE COMMUNITY GALA

A festive community bring and buy sale is on the go. Maybe there's an actual tombola happening as well with the audience winning prizes. Everything is festive and cheery but with an underlying competitive tension.

LJ. *(to the audience)* Our band might be banned but the gala wasn't all bad. 40% proof orange squash, five pounds in my pocket and buying back all my toys that mum'd tried to clear out. Marshmallows dipped in chocolate with smarties on top. Rice Krispie cakes and toffee apples.

TUCK. Look! LJ! My pineapple upside down cake took first prize.

LJ. No doubt!

TUCK. Where's Scarlett? I wanna rub her face in it.

PUBLIC HUMILIATION

SCARLETT comes in shaking gross water from her hands.

LJ. What happened to you?

SCARLETT. My stupid sister. Showing off to her knuckleheaded friends. Dunked my tarot cards in the toilet and flushed. Sarge just stood by and watched. I hate my sister and I hate Sarge.

TUCK. Why does everyone who isn't us suck monkey butt? Have some cake.

SCARLETT. Thanks, bud. Any sign of Robin?

TUCK. Not yet. Reckon she's chickened out?

LJ. She'll be here.

THE TOURNAMENT

SARGE speaks over a tannoy.

SARGE. The Corporation welcomes you to the Greenwood Gala. The Beautiful Baby contest has ended in a tie. We're now attempting to untangle the babies.

ROBIN enters, hood up, swaggering with sunglasses on, a backpack slung over her shoulder. She peeks in.

ROBIN. Hey, Pipsqueak. You remember the plan?

The backpack gives two flashes.

ROBIN. Excellent.

ROBIN drops in a couple a couple of sweets.

ROBIN. Hang tight, little buddy.

SARGE. We gently remind you that all unaccompanied minors will be forcibly removed from this Corporation provided Family Fun Day. Keep your eyes open for the young female known locally as Robin Hood. The Corporation wishes to speak to her regarding a recent theft of a very important wrist based whatjamacallit and certainly will NOT be boiling her ear lobes and using them as chewing gum. Okay, Greenwood, it says here that it's time for the big event. The 15th Annual Darts Tournament. Winner goes home with a deluxe, all in one karaoke and disco set. RRP £49.99 available from Argos in the centre. "Sing your song to the stars!" *(SARGE.'s eyes light up)* As me, myself and I will now be competing this afternoon, someone had better -

SARGE drops the mic to run over to the karaoke machine. Caressing it, she tries to figure out how darts work. TUCK runs up to the tannoy.

TUCK. Good morning, Greenwood! You join us today for the 15th Annual Darts championship here in Greenwood Community Hall. This historic title has been held by the Hood family for the past ten years. With none of them here today, this could be anybody's game. First up, someone who needs no introduction...

No one steps up, not sure what she means.

TUCK. Sarge. Sarge it's you m'am.

SARGE steps up to the mark and throws her darts at the board. She's unexpectedly good.

TUCK. A solid start there, setting the bar high. But can she be beaten?

SCARLETT, LJ and ROBIN step forward.

SARGE. May I remind you all that I play for the honour of The Corporation - who have complete power over the homes, wellbeing and livelihoods of you and your loved ones.

SCARLETT and LJ shrink back.

SARGE. No challengers. Looks like I win by default.

ROBIN. I challenge you!

TUCK. But wait - a mysterious stranger comes to test their hand at the game.

SARGE sees through ROBIN's "disguise" but decides to play along.

SARGE. All minors fourteen and under must be accompanied.

ROBIN. Check my bus pass.

ROBIN flicks out her pass with a flourish.

SARGE. You expect me to accept this damp cardboard? Judge! Disqualification!

TUCK comes over and looks at the pass.

TUCK. This is good for two more rides. I'll allow it.

SARGE. This place is out of control! Let's see how good you really are.

TUCK. Challenger! Take up your position.

ROBIN takes two shots. Two very good shots. The crowd cheer her on. SARGE is getting sick of it.

SARGE. You can't hoodwink me, Hood.

SARGE grabs ROBIN by the scruff and pulls her in.

LJ. Leave her alone.

SARGE pauses when she pulls off a pink bit of fluff stuck to Robin's top.

SARGE. Now now, what's this?

ROBIN. Cat barfed on me.

SARGE. You don't have a cat. You don't have anybody. I paid a visit to your registered address. Not a soul there.

ROBIN shrugs.

SARGE. You know more than you're letting on, Hood. I'm taking you in and your gonna tell me everything.

SCARLETT. Community Hall is sacred territory, Sarge.

TUCK. Neutral ground!

SARGE. Not anymore. The Corporation owns this town. I'll turn this place upside down to get to the heart of the trouble here. Come with me.

ROBIN. I've still got one more throw.

SARGE. Playtime's over.

ROBIN. Scared I might beat ya?

SARGE. Take your best shot, bub.

ROBIN. I will.

SARGE. Good.

ROBIN. Good.

SARGE. I'm glad.

ROBIN. Me too.

> *ROBIN lines up to take her shot. Everything goes in slow motion as her dart soars through the air.*

LJ. *(to the audience)* What happened next went down in Greenwood legend. Some folks say that Robin's darts flew through the air like shots of gold. Some say she broke the sound barrier with one hell of a throw. Some say that she tore up the board with a 180 her ancestors would have been proud of. The story I tell is something much more spectacular from my spectacular friend.

TUCK. By the power of Greyskull! She's only gone and split Sarge's dart in half!

SARGE. What?!

> *Everyone cheers as ROBIN waves her fists in the air. A chant goes up, taunting SARGE - "who are ya who are ya who are ya'.*

SARGE. No. No! Inconceivable! She cheated! You're coming with me!

ROBIN. Pipsqueak! Now!

The lights go frantic. The karaoke disco machine flashes on an off. Anything electrical goes nuts. Screaming and running and chaos! In the midst of it all, SARGE lunges at ROBIN, pulling their hood off.

SARGE. How did you do that?

But it's not ROBIN! It's SCARLETT.

SARGE. No! Where are you, Hood!

SARGE is pulling the hoods off all the kids now in the chaos. During the madness, all of the gang have switched into ROBIN disguises.

ROBIN. Yo. Barf breath. Over here!

ROBIN is standing triumphant with the karaoke machine, disguise cast off. Or maybe even cockily wearing SARGE's glasses. She grabs a dart from the board and lobs it at SARGE - it lands square in SARGE's bum. SARGE roars. A game of SARGE-in-the-middle starts with all the kids getting the better of SARGE.

SARGE. Impossible. You pathetic meat bags don't have the power to pull this off. What're you hiding!

A FIGHT WITH STICKS

SARGE grabs something from the Bring-n-Buy stall and brandishes it at ROBIN.

SARGE. Choose your weapon, punk.

ROBIN. Who woke up today and chose violence with their Cheerios?

SARGE. En guarde!

> *Over the course of this battle, the weapons are swapped out for increasingly more ludicrous things. Maybe it starts out as golf clubs or umbrellas, then its draught excluders or breadsticks, until they're fighting with cocktail sticks plucked from a cheese and pineapple hedgehog. ROBIN is having a blast whilst SARGE is getting more and more infuriated.*

ROBIN. You fight like my aunt.

SARGE. How strange you fight like an ant.

ROBIN. What?

SARGE. Like, a little, creature, bug.

ROBIN. Your aunt's an insect.

SARGE. No. You're an insect. Worm!

TUCK. So who's the ant?

SCARLETT. Her aunt's an ant.

TUCK. Got it.

LJ. I'm totally lost.

SARGE. Silence!

ROBIN. Never!

> *ROBIN screams as she lunges in again. They fight fluidly. It's quite an effort for SARGE but ROBIN makes it look effortless. Maybe ROBIN is making light sabre noises.*

SARGE. Is everything a game for you?

ROBIN. You're no fun.

SARGE. Why won't you die!

ROBIN. Give it up, poodle head.

> *SARGE lunges at ROBIN with the pointy end of a cocktail sausage. ROBIN makes a leap for it up onto the table whilst the rest of the gang tie SARGE up in the hazard tape previously used on the gang hut.*

SARGE. I hate you, Robin Hood!

ROBIN. And we were getting along so well. Ta ra, Sarge, it's been a real slice.

ESCAPING THE GALA

> *ROBIN has grabbed a cake from one of the stalls.*

TUCK. My prize cake! Noooo.

> *Maybe this bit goes in slow motion until - wham! ROBIN smacks it right into SARGE's face. ROBIN makes a dash for it, taking the karaoke machine with her as everyone cheers - 'Who are ya'.*

ROBIN. You're finally good for something, Tuck! Your prize cake saved the day!

> *In the celebration, PIPSQUEAK's bag is glowing. SARGE stares at it. The gang rush out triumphant. SARGE wipes the cream from her face. Fuming. Suspicious. She storms to the tannoy. Her voice booms out as the gang rush out.*

SARGE. I won't forget this, Hood! You've just made this personal. This is big time, baby!

> *SARGE speaks into her walkie talkie.*

SARGE. Sargent to Control. Sargent to Control. Send in The Big Guns. No kid gives Sarge the runaround. I'll tear through this hall, those woods, the horrible little houses filled with horrible little people. It's time Greenwood learnt how to handle a little authority.

HERE COME THE BIG GUNS

From the back of the stage, we see the looming figures of THE BIG GUNS - forbidding figures dressed in hazmat suits, faces obscured and a frightening heavy breathing.

ACT 2

A GREAT FEAST

If it's even possible, the den looks even more awesome than before. It's been electrified! Lights, noise and things spinning all over the place. Someone is making microwave popcorn and pop tarts. Someone's getting wrapped up giddily in Christmas tree lights. Disco ball is spinning and PIPSQUEAK is looking damn cool in a pair of sunglasses, pumping it's little bitty feet to the beat. It's an absolute ball. A sight of plenty. LJ's giving us an MTV style 'Cribs' tour. The others are enjoying mugging for the camera.

LJ. *(to audience)* Unlimited power! With our new friend, it was all of our Christmases and birthdays come at once! Games and sweets and all the good stuff. Best of all - freedom! Back home my folks were having to deal with dull parts of the holidays. Visiting elderly relatives. Obligatory religious festivals. Endless tedious, "work parties" - which is an oxymoron if there ever was one. But out here we were free. Who cares if it's dark by three in the afternoon - we had PIP POWER!

TUCK. Yo, Pip, my dude. Pump up the music!

A SINGSONG

TUCK. And now, people and Pipsqueaks of our beautiful Greenwood. Give it up for the musical stylings of Senior Robertoito of the Hooooooood!

ROBIN. Here's one for all the lovers out there.

The gang get into a very heartfelt and very silly rendition of the Bryan Adam's banger Everything I Do (I Do It for You). A proper party, heartfelt, energetic and carefree.

Right at the peak of the fun, the music starts speeding as PIPSQUEAK attempts to keep up with the pace of the gang. He can't keep it up and the music slows to a low crawl before cutting out.

PIP GETS SICK

TUCK. Aww. What happened to the tunes?

SCARLETT. Guys, is Pip looking a little low in life-force to you?

LJ. Maybe it's past his bedtime.

ROBIN. He's fine. Give him some Fizz Wiz and he'll perk up again.

LJ. He needs to rest.

ROBIN attempts to pour sugar on PIPSQUEAK.

SCARLETT. Careful, too much sugar can clog the chakras. Don't want him to end up getting a complex over their M&Ms like Tuck.

TUCK. What's that supposed to mean?

ROBIN. Means you can be a real cry baby when it comes to your candy.

SCARLETT. I did Pip's cards. He'll be right as rain tomorrow. Can't party all night.

ROBIN. Oh let's not go home yet.

LJ. He'll be better in the morning.

The gang start to pack up for the night. ROBIN attempts to stop them.

ROBIN. Hey hey - did you see the look on Sarge's face when I got her right in the smacker?

TUCK. I couldn't make it out for all of the double piped chantilly cream dripping from her chin...

LJ. It's cold. Let's go home.

SCARLETT. Freezing without Pip.

ROBIN. Just one more, it's still early.

ROBIN. shakes on some more sweeties. The music briefly comes back on.

ROBIN. There you go. No problemo.

PIPSQUEAK sparks and the music and lights burn out again.

SCARLETT. Muy problemo, senor.

LJ. Smells like burnt toast.

ROBIN. What we need is a plan -

*TUCK has opened up all her sweets and dumped them on
PIPSQUEAK. He goes into overdrive, everything going crazy.*

ROBIN. Take cover!

PIPSQUEAK rattles and shakes and everything totally blows.

ROBIN. What have you done?

SCARLETT. Tuck!

LJ. I think Pip's going to vom.

ROBIN. Way to go, genius.

TUCK. What did I do?

ROBIN. You blew up Pip, idiot.

TUCK. I was trying to help.

SCARLETT. She was only copying you, Rob.

ROBIN. Yeah, well maybe the dork should get her own act and quit
blowing up our friends.

THE GANG GET INTO A FIGHT

TUCK. Why am I always the one getting my buns busted? Why don't we ride on LJ for a bit?

LJ. What have I done?

ROBIN. *(to Tuck)* Leave LJ alone. Give Pip some space. You're crowding him.

TUCK. You don't get to tell me what to do.

ROBIN. Yes I do. You'd never have any fun if it wasn't for me. Letting that Corporation kill joy walk all over you. "Yes, ma'am. No, ma'am." Pathetic.

TUCK. Well, your last "fun" totally trashed my prize cake.

ROBIN. And I think you'll find it was hilarious.

LJ. Guys... Pip's got a fever.

TUCK. You're a trouble maker, Robin. My dad -

ROBIN. Get some new material, bub.

TUCK. My dad -

ROBIN. Yeah?

TUCK. My dad says -

ROBIN. Spit it out.

TUCK. My dad says you've turned into a sadistic, worthless, no good, bigmouth, know-it-all, latchkey bully.

SCARLETT. Ouch...

LJ. *(about Pipsqueak)* Guys.

ROBIN. Why are you hanging round then? Go home to your boring old man and his gross spaghetti.

SCARLETT. Ooooookay....

LJ. *(about Pipsqueak)* This is serious.

SCARLETT. Let's just breathe. We're all just feeling a bit emotional because Mercury's -

ROBIN. Live in the real world for once, space cadet.

LJ. Guys. Pip's really not well.

SCARLETT. Real world? Come on, Robin.

ROBIN. What?

SCARLETT. You've hardly spoken about your folks.

TUCK. Everyone know's they're sick, Robin.

ROBIN. Think I care about that? They were always trying to get me to stay inside when there was all this thisness to explore out here.

TUCK. Have you even been to see them in the hospital?

SCARLETT. I bet you she hasn't.

ROBIN. Because you can see all that can you, oh Scarlett the great and mystical.

SCARLETT. Well, have you?

ROBIN. Know what I see in your future?

SCARLETT. Rob -

ROBIN. Office cubicle. Strip lights. Shackled to mediocracy.

LJ. Guys!

ROBIN. What do you want, LJ? Can't you leave me alone for one minute

LJ. Always running your mouth, Robin, but you never actually say anything.

ROBIN. What do you want me to say?

LJ. How you feel. How you really feel.

ROBIN. I feel. I feel like you're all killing my buzz.

LJ. Take some responsibility for own emotions!

ROBIN. If I wanted responsibility I would have stayed in the city.

LJ. Whatever. I'm going home.

ROBIN. If you go home now, LJ, we're done. I swear it.

LJ. It's not just Tuck's dad who thinks you've turned into a bully.

ROBIN. Oh yeah?

LJ. I think you are too.

ROBIN. A bully. That what you really think, LJ?

LJ. Pipsqueak needs help.

ROBIN. Fine. I'll help him. I'll take some of your brilliant "responsibility". On my own. I'm going solo. Robin and the Mystery Machine? Donezo.

TUCK. Fine by me.

LJ. Fine!

SCARLETT. The pact's a bunch of hocus pocus anyway.

ROBIN. I'm taking my fur ball and I'm going home.

TUCK. You don't have a home!

> *ROBIN shoves PIPSQUEAK in a backpack and storms off. The rest of the gang look guiltily at each other.*

LJ. We took it to far.

SCARLETT. Where's she going to go?

TUCK. I don't care.

SCARLETT. Yeah you do.

TUCK. Yeah. I do.

SCARLETT. Come on.

LJ. Are we going after her?

SCARLETT. No, let's just go home. C'mon, Tuck. I'll help you make a new cake.

AMBUSH!

LJ. *(to the audience)* I felt trash leaving Robin alone. She had Pipsqueak, sure. But sometimes you need a hand to hold. That night, I shovelled my dinner as fast as I could, snuck back to the gang hut, pockets full of pudding. I was going to find Robin and say "I'm sorry", things were more fun with her around. She's the only one who gets me. I was going to make it up to her, I was going to -

> *LJ is cut off sharply by A BIG GUN who has come up behind her and grabbed her hands behind her back. SARGE leaps from the bushes.*

SARGE. Fools! That's the wrong one! However… She might do. Take her away!

THE BIG GUNS bundle LJ off with SARGE sweeping the area behind her. ROBIN peeks on from a hiding place, PIPSQUEAK simpering under her arm. She shushes him.

ROBIN. What do you expect me to do? There's loads of them and only one of me.

PIPSQUEAK whimpers.

ROBIN. I'm scared too, buddy.

BLINDFOLDED & BOUND

LJ is tied to a chair in the community centre. Her hands are bound behind her. She struggles and fights against her bindings. THE BIG GUNS stand over her, silent and menacing.

SARGE. So. Kid. You've tried my patience. You've got something I want. Talk!

LJ makes some kind of gesture to indicate that she can't really talk if her hands are tied behind her back.

SARGE. Untie her.

THE BIG GUNS release her bonds. LJ rubs them painfully. SARGE leans down over her.

SARGE. Now tell me - ow!

LJ has bopped her in the face. LJ shakes her fist. That hurt more than expected. THE BIG GUNS step in to defend SARGE.

SARGE. No. I can handle her. I've given you your hands back. I can play nice. Will you play with me?

LJ makes a rude hand gesture.

SARGE. Real smart, yes. Don't you forget who has got who tied up at their mercy, girly. My buddies aren't quite so friendly as me.

LJ. Fine.

SARGE. Now we're on the same side, you're going to help me. This troop leader of yours? Where's she keeping the source of her power? Just who is Robin Hood?

LJ. She's my friend.

SARGE. Is that it?

LJ. That's all you're getting.

TORTURE

SARGE. Oh I've been watching. Learning. I know your weaknesses. I've seen what makes your kind talk... TICKLE THE PRISONER!

> *THE BIG GUNS set about LJ. It's terrifying tickle torture. It's like she's being electrocuted.*

LJ. Stop Stop!

SARGE. You ready to talk?

LJ. I'll spill. I'll spill.

SARGE. Good girl.

LJ. Just not in front of them.

SARGE. Leave us!

> *THE BIG GUNS hesitate.*

SARGE. Move your shiny butts outta my office!

> *THE BIG GUNS bump into each other in their rush to leave.*

SARGE. Cosy.

LJ. Why do you have it in for us?

SARGE. You've taken something from me. Something very important. And if I can't do my job... what am I good for?

LJ places a sympathetic hand on Sarge.

LJ. You're trying your best.

SARGE. What are you doing? Get your hands of me, filthy specimen! Someone needs to call your parents. And that someone. Is me!

LJ. Noooooooooooooooo!

The sound of breaking glass alerts SARGE. Her attention is diverted.

SARGE. I've got a phone call to make.

ROBIN SAVES THE DAY

ROBIN creeps in.

ROBIN. LJ!

LJ. No! Get outta here!

ROBIN. I'm so sorry. I shouldn't have blown up at you all like that.

LJ. It doesn't matter.

ROBIN. You're shivering? What did that monster do to you?

LJ. Felt like being electrocuted. But it's nothing.

ROBIN. She's not right. Everything's been so crap since I was shipped to the city. Been sleeping in the hut just to get out of having to go back there.

LJ. Will you shut up and listen for once.

ROBIN. Woah. Of course.

LJ. Sarge knows we've been stealing from her. She knows about Pipsqueak. And now, she's got the whole of The Corporation out looking for us.

TAKING THE HIT

LJ. The gang's in danger. She's going to call our parents.

ROBIN. Oh geez. We need to get you home, quick.

LJ. Mum is gonna kill me. I'll never be allowed to hang out with you guys after this.

> *ROBIN firmly pulls LJ up.*

ROBIN. I'll take the heat.

LJ. You can't.

ROBIN. Everyone knows I'm a lousy latchkey brat with a big mouth and no future. You're the good kids.

> *BIG GUNS appear and loom over them. Arms stretched out like zombies. Heavy breathing.*

ROBIN. Oh my god!

LJ. We're dead!

ROBIN. Never say die! Let's show them how Greenwood fights back!

> *ROBIN and LJ strike action poses.*

A DARING RESCUE

Laughter and giggles emerge from under the suits. TUCK and SCARLETT take off their helmets.

LJ. You scared us to death.

ROBIN. What are you doing!

SCARLETT. Being a couple of real good kids.

ROBIN. Urg. You heard that did you.

SCARLETT. Very moving.

TUCK. My dad says he's sorry he was mean do you.

SCARLETT. Your dad?

TUCK. I say I'm sorry I was mean to you.

LJ. How did you get in?

SCARLETT. Treated those goons to some of Tuck's prize pineapple upside down cake.

TUCK. Laced with Scarlett's barftastic berries.

SCARLETT. Their stomachs couldn't stand it.

TUCK. There was a typhoon of spew!

SCARLETT. The Awesome Twosome.

TUCK. Here to save your butts!

LJ. You guys are brilliant.

ROBIN. Seems like you don't need me after all.

TUCK. You kidding? We freaked out when you guys weren't back at the den.

SCARLETT. But we centered our spirits and asked -

TUCK. What would Robin do?

ROBIN. You've done me proud guys.

TUCK. I love you guys.

LJ. I love YOU guys!

SCARLETT. Leave all that peace and harmony to me. Can we please get moving?

SARGE creeps into the room, a wicked grin on her face.

SARGE. Hello, children.

TUCK. Where did she spring from?

ROBIN. We're not afraid of you!

SARGE. We is it now, you plural punks? I could tell you were here as soon as I smelt the bubblegum. It's time to put an end to this.

ROBIN pulls PIPSQUEAK out of the backpack and brandishes it at SARGE like a weapon. SARGE stares in disbelief.

ROBIN. Pip! Hit the lights.

The lights flash a little but stay resolutely on.

TUCK. Pip's out of juice!

SARGE. *(booming)* What have you done!

ROBIN. There's only one thing left for it.

SCARLETT. What?

ROBIN. Ruuuuuuuuuuuuun!

CHASE THROUGH THE NIGHT

The gang are running through the trees. It's dark and shadows of trees and bodies flash by. Torches race past. It's disorienting and thrilling. We catch flashes of people running back and forth as THE BIG GUNS chase down the gang.

SCARLETT "DIES".

SCARLETT falls over and twists her ankle.

SCARLETT. Ahh! Go on without me!

ROBIN. No way.

TUCK. It's too late!

LJ. Sarge is coming!

SCARLETT. I'm finished. At last I fall into the sweet release of death.

SCARLETT dramatically faints away.

TUCK. Scarlett! Noooo! Not like this. I should be the one to kill you!

ROBIN. LJ. Get over here and help Scarlett get on my back.

TUCK. Oh, can I get a co-carry too?

ROBIN. You're not injured!

TUCK. I'm upset!

LJ has helped SCARLETT up. ROBIN picks her up and puts her on her back

ROBIN. Someone grab Pipsqueak and lets book!

UNDER SEIGE

The gang have made it back to the hide out. Panting and worse for wear. LJ is examining PIPSQUEAK.

LJ. Pipsqueak can't take any more, Robin.

TUCK. Neither can I.

SCARLETT. Why did we think we could take on The Corporation and win?

ROBIN looks around at her troops, they look defeated.

ROBIN. Guys. We had a good run.

The gang huddle close to one another. THE BIG GUNS surround them, filling the stage with fog. SARGE speaks to them over a megaphone.

SARGE. The Corporation has tried to be fair. The Corporation has tried to be kind. The Corporation will resort to force.

ROBIN. And if it's gonna end, this is how I'd want to go. We might not come back from this one alive, but nothing that doesn't come with a side order pain is any fun. I hope my bruises never fade. Cause each one is a badge of honour. Proof that I pushed myself a little further. Ran faster. Climbed higher. Took life on face first.

ALL. Yeah!

ROBIN. Now. Who wants to get skint knees with me!

The gang are ready themselves for the end. LJ holds them back.

SACRIFICING YOURSELF

LJ. Stop. You stay here. I'll go.

TUCK. No!

SCARLETT. Your mum will go spare.

LJ. I know.

ROBIN. You don't have to do this, LJ

LJ. I want to.

> *LJ steps out in front of SARGE, growing more confident with each step she takes. PIPSQUEAK in the bag glows stronger and stronger.*

SARGE. Good girl.

> *LJ, arms splayed out, chin to the sky. Radiant in her martyrdom.*

SARGE. Open. The. Backpack.

LJ. Huh?

RETURN OF THE KING

> *SARGE strips her face off. Or maybe takes her gloves off and her skin is fuzzy and neon. She's a shining glowing alien. Like a big version of PIPSQUEAK.*

ROBIN. Who *are* you?

SCARLETT. Wait a minute. It's her. The power cuts started as soon as she arrived on the scene. She's...

ALL. The Beast of Greenwood!

SARGE. I've come for the King.

*The gang all look around. PIPSQUEAK, the king, shudders
and squeaks at SARGE in recognition.*

SARGE. I have missed you my liege.

TUCK. Mother of Mothra! A king!

ROBIN. What does that make Pip - your kid?

SARGE. I would be honoured to be related to such a noble one
as he. I'm his... babysitter.

ALL. A babysitter?!

SARGE. Bow before the King.

> *TUCK bows down low to PIPSQUEAK. The others follow, but
> ROBIN stands resolute in front of SARGE.*

ROBIN. We don't do royalty round here. Greenwood's a
democracy.

SARGE. Really?

ROBIN. Well, someone has to be in charge...

> *PIPSQUEAK flashes and beeps.*

SARGE. My master tells me you have been a friend to him?

ROBIN. Of course. He's one of the gang.

SARGE. You are not... the enemy...?

TUCK. You're the one whose been hounding us.

LJ. We're sorry, Pip got sick.

TUCK. We didn't know what to do.

SARGE. Have you tried turning him on and off again?

Whoever is holding PIPSQUEAK tips him upside down. He makes the noise of a computer restarting.

TUCK. Rad!

SARGE. Please don't tell his parents I lost track of this regal trouble maker.

SCARLETT. Your secrets safe with us.

SARGE. I'll put in a good word for you with The Corporation. The next Greenwood Gala will need a musical act should you wish to take the gig...

LJ. Oh course we want the gig!

ROBIN. I dunno...

SCARLETT. Rob, come on.

ROBIN. It's... I don't mind if you drop my name from the posters. 'The Mystery Machine' is cool enough for all of us.

ALL. Amazing! Brilliant! Neat!

SARGE. I need to get this one back home.

ROBIN. Where will you go?

SARGE settles PIPSQUEAK in her trolley.

SARGE. I'll transfer my commission to our home planet. We will sail to Mercury.

SCARLETT. I knew it!

SARGE. *(holding a hand out to Robin)* I believe you have something belonging to me.

ROBIN pulls SARGE's watch from her pocket. SARGE puts it on and presses a button. The lights from her space ship burst into action.

SARGE. The time for conflict is over. My lord. It's time to come in for your dinner.

The gang huddle round PIPSQUEAK.

ROBIN. Friends for life. Until the end of the universe. No matter how far. Right guys?

ALL. Right.

SARGE takes PIPSQUEAK from them.

SARGE. Thank you. Friends.

PIPSQUEAK squeaks and whines.

PIPSQUEAK. Be good.

ROBIN, LJ, SCARLETT and TUCK all bow in respect to PIPSQUEAK and SARGE.

AN INVITATION TO DINNER

The gang stand holding and hugging one another as SARGE and PIPSQUEAK exit. A huge gust of wind and an awesome lightning flash as their space craft rises for take off.

ROBIN runs forward and calls up.

ROBIN. Wait!

SARGE. What!

ROBIN. Do you guys want to stay for tea? ... We've got cake.

SARGE. Oh. Yes. I think we would.

The spaceship gets parked up. Beep beep. Like a Volvo being remotely locked.

AN ENDING?

LJ. Good times don't last forever. One more Christmas and the band would be broken up for good. Scarlett found fortune running a shamanic pop up shop up The Center. Tuck and her dad rose to fame winning the Bake Off as the first father/daughter team. Me, I was the greatest betrayer. I got a boyfriend. When love lost its luster, I came back home to the hut. But Robin was gone. Some said her folks got better and they all moved on. Some say her gran brought her back to the city. I say Pipsqueak and his family brought her back home with them. At least, that's the story I choose to tell.

WOODLAND WEDDING

There is food and lights and cake and everything all around. It's a big celebration.

TUCK. Okay. Here's the deal. You swear to the pact badda bing badda boom, then we all get to eat. Everyone gets an equal share.

SCARLETT. Everyone has a good time, all the time.

ROBIN. No one gets left behind.

LJ. Friends until the end of the universe.

ALL. I pledge allegiance to the flag. To always help others and do my best. To boldly go where no one has gone before. By the power of Greyskull. Thunder, thunder, thunder, Thundercats ho.

ROBIN. I now pronounce you an official member of The Mystery Machine. Forever and ever. Amen.

ALL. Amen.

They smile and shove cake in each other's mouths.

DANCING WITH THE ENEMY

ROBIN. Shall we retire to the lounge for the entertainment? Who is up first?

TUCK. Oh, me, Robin, pick me, pick me, pick me.

ROBIN. No, anyone? Anyone?

TUCK is dancing in her seat arms up.

ROBIN. Oh you go, Tuck.

TUCK. Yeeeeeeees.

The gang show off their turns. These party pieces can be swapped around. Maybe burping the alphabet. Dislocating arms. Maybe SCARLETT does some scary performance poetry. ROBIN turns to SARGE.

ROBIN. What about you, ma'am?

LJ. I think she's chicken.

SARGE. I am nobody's chicken, m'am.

The gang all start clucking and flapping their wings.

SARGE. Alright! Quit your squalling. I haven't done it in some time. I might be a bit rusty.

The gang all settle down expectedly, eyes wide and excited for what their guest might pull out of the bag. SARGE composes herself. Stands as pin straight as an Irish dancer. With an absolutely straight face, she starts to jerk and spasm unnaturally. The gang are a bit perturbed at first but as SARGE continues with her performance with a stony face, it becomes clear that SARGE is performing an absolute pitch perfect, storming performance of the 'Thriller' dance. The gang cheer her on and hum along the tune. The more into it they get, the more we start to see a smile creep up on SARGE's face. The glee builds to a crescendo as they leap to their feet and join in SARGE's dance - picking up moves here and there.

SCARLETT. Pipsqueak! Play 'Thriller'! One, two, three, four!

PIPSQUEAK bursts into a high pitched and adorable version of 'Thriller' as the stage bursts and pulses with colour. It's a wild, fabulous, furiously silly time.

LJ. *(to the audience)* I live in that moment forever. Me and my friends. Eternal. Until the end of the universe.

THE END.

Eve Nicol is a Glaswegian playwright and director.

Her plays include *If You're Feeling Sinister [a play with songs]* with Stuart Murdoch and Belle & Sebastian, and *One Life Stand*, published by Oberon Books.

Her work as a director includes world premieres of new plays for the Traverse Theatre and National Theatre of Scotland, as well as work with Royal Lyceum Theatre, Edinburgh and Tron Theatre, Glasgow.